VISIT US AT
www.abdopublishing.com

Published by ABDO Publishing Company, 8000 West 78th Street, Edina, Minnesota 55439.

Copyright © 2010 by Abdo Consulting Group, Inc. International copyrights reserved in all countries. No part of this book may be reproduced in any form without written permission from the publisher. Buddy Books™ is a trademark and logo of ABDO Publishing Company.

Printed in the United States of America, North Mankato, Minnesota.
112009
012010

PRINTED ON RECYCLED PAPER

Coordinating Series Editor: Rochelle Baltzer
Editor: Sarah Tieck
Contributing Editors: Heidi M.D. Elston, Megan M. Gunderson, BreAnn Rumsch, Marcia Zappa
Graphic Design: Deborah Coldiron, Maria Hosley
Cover Photograph: *Eighth Street Studio*; *iStockphoto*: ©iStockphoto.com/Benjiecce, ©iStockphoto.com/Rouzes.
Interior Photographs/Illustrations: *Eighth Street Studio* (pp. 7, 11, 13, 26, 30); *iStockphoto*: ©iStockphoto.com/alexKoen (p. 21), ©iStockphoto.com/AndreyTTL (p. 13), ©iStockphoto.com/bonniej (p. 16), ©iStockphoto.com/cglade (p. 26), ©iStockphoto.com/johnandersonphoto (p. 25), ©iStockphoto.com/Maica (p. 29), ©iStockphoto.com/mammamaart (p. 29), ©iStockphoto.com/stockcam (p. 5); *Minden Pictures*: Piotr Naskrecki (p. 11); *Peter Arnold, Inc.*: Michel Gunther (p. 8), Cal Vornberger (p. 5), Wittek, R. (p. 7); *Photo Researchers, Inc.*: ©Kenneth H. Thomas (p. 25); *Photos.com*: Jupiter Images (p. 15); *Shutterstock*: asharkyu (p. 14), Rusty Dodson (p. 5), Frances L. Fruit (p. 29), Kletr (p. 19), Hannu Liivar (p. 14), Lilya (p. 23), Steffen Foerster Photography (p. 8), Tijmen (p. 14), Caroline Tolsma (p. 17), worldswildlifewonders (pp. 5, 8), Michael Zysman (pp. 19, 29).

Library of Congress Cataloging-in-Publication Data

Murray, Julie, 1969-
  Slowest animals / Julie Murray.
    p. cm. -- (That's wild! : a look at animals)
 ISBN 978-1-60453-979-0
 1. Animal locomotion--Juvenile literature. 2. Speed--Juvenile literature. I. Title.
 QP301.M743 2010
 590--dc22
                                                        2009034357

Contents

Wildly Slow! 4
Sleepy Sloth 6
Spit It Out 10
A Snail's Pace 12
Slowpoke 16
A Horse Is a Horse 20
Slow Birds 22
Crawling Along 27
That WAS Wild! 28
Wow! Is That TRUE? 30
Important Words 31
Web Sites 31
Index 32

Wildly Slow!

Gila Monster

Many amazing animals live in our world. Some are big and others are small. They may fly, run, or swim.

Some animals are wildly slow! Their slow speed can help them survive in their **habitats**. Being slow might help them sneak up on **prey** or hide from predators. Let's learn more about slow animals!

Sloth

Sleepy Sloth

The sloth is a slow-moving **mammal**. It hangs upside down from tree branches. The sloth has weak back legs. So, it uses its arms and claws to move.

A sloth's slow speed **protects** it from predators, such as jaguars and harpy eagles. Usually, predators don't even notice a sloth in the trees. If predators do see it, the sloth protects itself by clawing.

Can You Believe It?

Sloths are good swimmers!

Sloths live in tropical rain forests in Central and South America.

7

Can you see the baby sloth? They often cling to their mothers.

Most sloths look a little bit green. They move so slowly that algae grows on their fur!

It is hard for sloths to move on the ground. They use their arms to drag themselves along.

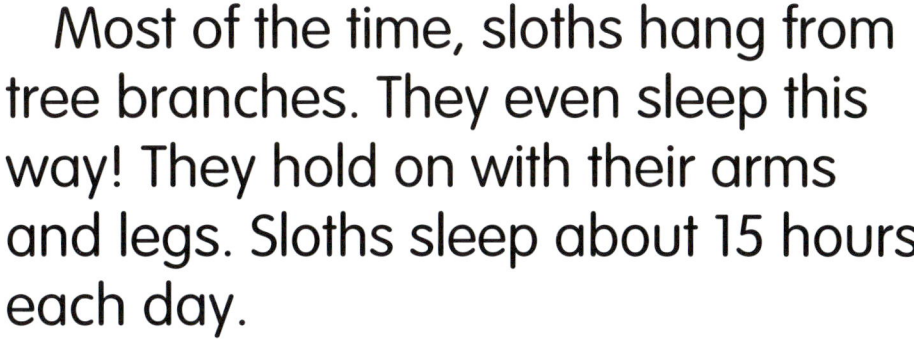

Most of the time, sloths hang from tree branches. They even sleep this way! They hold on with their arms and legs. Sloths sleep about 15 hours each day.

Sloths are most active at night. When it is time to eat, they climb slowly through the branches. They move hand over hand to search for fruits, leaves, and twigs.

Spit It Out

Beautiful Backs
The spitting spider has markings on its back. They remind some people of Chinese writing.

Most spiders move quickly to attack. But, spitting spiders slowly sneak up on their **prey**. When the spider is about one-half inch (1 cm) away, it spits poisonous silk.

The spider spits from side to side. It covers its prey in a zigzag line of sticky silk. The silk traps the prey. This takes less than one second! The spitting spider may move slow, but it acts fast!

Spitting spiders catch spiders, flies, and other insects to eat.

11

Some snails grow less than one inch (3 cm) long. Others reach two feet (1 m) in length!

A Snail's Pace

Snails are famous for their slow speed. They may travel less than three inches (8 cm) per minute!

A snail moves on a **muscular** body part called a foot. Its foot spreads out under its body. To move, a snail **flexes** and shifts its foot. As it slides along, its body lets out **mucus**. This helps the snail move more easily.

It's All in the Name
Snails without shells are called slugs.

A snail's soft body is usually protected by a shell. The shell often has a circular shape called a spiral.

Watch Them Go

Scientists are studying snails. They want to create robots that can move on many different surfaces like snails do.

Snails may be slow, but they can move almost anywhere! Their **flexible** bodies allow them to move on many surfaces.

Snails live in areas as different as oceans and deserts. So, they may travel up trees or slide over rocks. Some can even move upside down on **ceilings**!

Old as Dirt
Giant tortoises may live more than 100 years!

Slowpoke

Like snails, turtles are famous for moving slowly. One of the slowest turtles is the giant tortoise. These animals live on land.

Giant tortoises can move over rocks and other uneven land. But, they move very slowly. They travel just three or four miles (5 or 6 km) in an entire day!

Giant tortoises live on the Galápagos and Aldabra islands.

Adult giant tortoises may weigh 500 pounds (230 kg)! They have strong bodies. Their hard shells **protect** them from predators.

Young giant tortoises are not as protected. Rats, dogs, and cats hunt them. These predators also eat tortoise eggs.

Baby giant tortoises hatch from eggs.

Some giant tortoises can go a whole year without eating or drinking. Their bodies are made to store enough food and water to survive.

A Horse Is a Horse

Sea horses are among the slowest swimmers. These unusual fish swim upright. They move so slowly it looks like they're just floating!

While moving, sea horses get hungry. Their bodies often match their surroundings. So, they hide in seaweed and coral. They wait for **plankton** and other small animals to pass by. Then, they suck them into their mouths!

Sometimes sea horses have trouble swimming in strong waves. They use their tails to hook onto seaweed and coral. This helps them stay in one place.

Slow Birds

Chickens are not built for speed. They have round bodies and small legs. Their wings only allow them to fly short distances.

These birds are known to walk slowly and proudly. This is called a strut. If they feel unsafe, chickens can run. Their top speed is about nine miles (14 km) per hour.

> Chickens live throughout the world. There are likely more chickens than any other type of bird.

Another slow bird is the American woodcock. It can fly as slow as five miles (8 km) per hour. That makes it the slowest-flying bird.

American woodcocks nest in the eastern United States and southern Canada. These round birds are often seen walking along the forest floor. They use their long beaks to find earthworms in the ground.

An American woodcock's eyes are far back on its head. This helps it see all the way around its body!

American woodcocks are mostly tan and brown. This matches their leafy surroundings, which helps them hide from predators.

Full Bellies

Gila monsters eat very large meals. They store fat in their bellies and tails. They survive on this fat for the winter.

Gila monsters are the largest lizards native to the United States.

Crawling Along

Like many lizards, the Gila monster travels at a crawling pace. Gila monsters live in desert areas. In warm weather, they move as little as possible. They hide out in underground dens.

Gila monsters prefer meals that don't move or move very little. This includes eggs. Then they don't have to chase their food!

That WAS wild!

From poky giant tortoises to sleepy sloths, there are some very slow wild animals. Each of them is an important part of the animal kingdom.

People work hard to **protect** animals and their surroundings. You can help, too! Recycling and using less water are two simple things you can do. The more you learn, the more you can do to help keep animals safe.

It is important to hike on established trails. This helps protect wild animal habitats.

Giant tortoises are in danger of dying out. But, scientists and other people work to protect them.

Planting a tree may provide some wild animals with a home.

Wow! Is That TRUE?

🐾 For most creatures, females have babies. But sea horse males give birth! The male sea horse carries the female's eggs in his pouch.

🐾 Gila monsters and Mexican beaded lizards are the only lizards known to make venom. When attacked, they bite and release this poison into predators.

🐾 In some parts of the world, people hold snail races.

Important Words

ceiling (SEE-lihng) the overhead, inside part of a room.

flex to bend. Something that is flexible bends easily.

habitat a place where a living thing is naturally found.

mammal a group of living beings. Mammals have hair and make milk to feed their babies.

mucus (MYOO-kuhs) thick, slippery, protective fluid from the body.

muscular (MUHS-kyuh-luhr) having strong, well-developed muscles. Muscles are body tissues, or layers of cells, that help move the body.

plankton tiny animals and plants that float in a body of water.

prey an animal hunted or killed by a predator for food.

protect (pruh-TEHKT) to guard against harm or danger.

Web Sites

To learn more about slow animals, visit ABDO Publishing Company online. Web sites about slow animals are featured on our Book Links page. These links are routinely monitored and updated to provide the most current information available.

www.abdopublishing.com

Index

Aldabra Islands **16**

American woodcock **5, 24, 25**

animal homes **27, 29**

Canada **24**

Central America **7**

chicken **22**

conservation **28, 29**

defense **4, 6, 18, 22, 25, 30**

eating habits **9, 11, 19, 20, 24, 26, 27**

enemies **4, 6, 18, 25, 30**

Galápagos Islands **16**

giant tortoise **5, 16, 18, 19, 28, 29**

Gila monster **4, 26, 27, 30**

habitats **4, 7, 15, 16, 24, 25, 27, 29**

hunting **4, 10, 11, 20, 27**

Mexican beaded lizard **30**

sea horse **20, 21, 30**

sloth **4, 6, 7, 8, 9, 28**

snail **12, 15, 16, 30**

South America **7**

spitting spider **10, 11**

United States **24, 27**